American Indian Nations

The Apache

Nomadic Hunters of the Southwest

by Mary Englar

Consultant:
Adella Swift
Apache Historian
San Carlos Apache
Peridot, Arizona

Capstone press

Mankato, Minnesota

Capstone Press,
151 Good Counsel Drive • P.O. Box 669 • Mankato, Minnesota 56002.
www.capstonepress.com

Copyright © 2003 by Capstone Press. All rights reserved.
No part of this publication may be reproduced in whole or in part, or stored in a retrieval system, or transmitted in any form or by any means, electronic, mechanical, photocopying, recording, or otherwise, without written permission of the publisher. For information regarding permission, write to Capstone Press, 151 Good Counsel Drive, P.O. Box 669, Dept. R, Mankato, Minnesota 56002.
Printed in the United States of America

Library of Congress Cataloging-in-Publication Data
Englar, Mary.
 The Apache: nomadic hunters of the Southwest / by Mary Englar.
 p. cm.—(American Indian nations)
 Summary: Looks at the customs, family life, history, government, culture, and daily life of the Apache people of Oklahoma, New Mexico, and Arizona.
 Includes bibliographical references and index.
 ISBN-13: 978-0-7368-1563-5 (hardcover)
 ISBN-10: 0-7368-1563-5 (hardcover)
 ISBN-13: 978-0-7368-4814-5 (softcover pbk.)
 ISBN-10: 0-7368-4814-2 (softcover pbk.)
 1. Apache Indians—Juvenile literature. [1. Apache Indians. 2. Indians of North America.] I. Title. II. American Indian nations series.
E99.A6 E64 2003
979.004'972—dc21   2002010365

Editorial Credits
 Bradley P. Hoehn and Christopher Harbo, editors; Kia Adams, designer and illustrator; Alta Schaffer, photo researcher; Karen Risch, product planning editor

Photo Credits
Art Resource/Werner Forman, 21
Capstone Press/Gary Sundermeyer, 17 (top right)
Corbis/Frederick Remington, 25; J. McDonald, 36–37
The Denver Public Library, 11, 30 (both)
Frank C. McCarthy/The Greenwich Workshop, Inc.,
 www.greenwichworkshop.com, 14–15
Houserstock/Dave G. Houser, 34; Jan Butchofsky, 45
Hulton Archive by Getty Images, 22–23
John Annerino (c) 2002, 19
Kit Breen, cover, 43 (top)
Marilyn "Angel" Wynn, 7, 8, 16–17, 32–33, 40
Place Stock Photo, cover inset, 4, 38, 41, 43 (bottom), 44
Stock Montage, Inc, 29
Will Sampson Jr./The Philbrook Museum of Art, Tulsa, OK, 27

1 2 3 4 5 6 08 07 06 05 04 03

Table of Contents

1 Who Are the Apache? 5
2 Traditional Life 9
3 Spanish and Americans Bring Change . . . 23
4 The Apache Today 31
5 Sharing the Traditions. 39

Features

Map: Apache Lands Past and Present 13
Recipe: Pine Nut Muffins 17
Apache Timeline 44
Glossary 46
For Further Reading 46
Places to Write and Visit 47
Internet Sites 47
Index 48

John Weldon Elementary
7370 Weldon Spring Road
Dardenne Prairie, MO 63368

Mescalero Apache dancers wear traditional clothing for the Apache Mescal Roast. The roast celebrates the traditional methods of cooking the mescal plant.

Chapter One

Who Are the Apache?

About 1,000 years ago, the Apache people left their homes in northwest Canada. They moved south into the Great Plains and the dry lands of the American Southwest. No one knows exactly when the Apache arrived in the Southwest, but Spanish explorers wrote about them in the 1500s. Today, more than 57,000 Apache live in Oklahoma, New Mexico, and Arizona.

Nomadic Life

The Apache were nomads. They often moved, searching for hunting areas, fresh water, and wild plants. The Apache homelands reached from Arizona through New Mexico and to Colorado, Oklahoma, and Texas. The Apache often crossed what is now the United States–Mexico border.

On their journeys, the Apache stopped to trade with other tribes. The Zuni Pueblo Indians called the Apache "apachu." This word means "stranger" or "enemy" in the Zuni language. The Spanish later changed this name to Apache. Apache called themselves Ndee or Inde (in-DAY), which means "the people."

The Apache preferred to live a free life. They did not settle into villages like the Pueblo Indians and the Spanish. The Apache hunted and gathered food in the dry canyons, river valleys, and mountains of their homelands. When they ran out of food, they raided their neighbors for cattle, horses, and corn. Their groups were small. After raids, they moved quickly into the mountains to escape from their enemies. This lifestyle allowed them to remain independent from the Spanish, Mexicans, and U.S. government for almost 300 years.

Apache Nation

Today, the Apache Nation is separated into the Western Apache of Arizona and the Eastern Apache of New Mexico and Oklahoma. The Western bands include the White Mountain, the San Carlos, and the Tonto Apache. The Eastern bands include the Kiowa-Apache, the Lipan, the Mescalero, the Jicarilla, and the Chiricahua Apache.

Modern Apache are employed in tourism, ranching, farming, and casinos. Some work as fire fighters and hunting guides. Years of war with the Spanish, Mexicans, and U.S. government almost destroyed the Apache way of life. The Apache are now growing and sharing their traditions, language, and lands with their children.

The Salt River Canyon separates the San Carlos Apache Reservation from the Fort Apache Reservation in Arizona.

The Western Apache lived in wickiups. Wickiups often were made of long wooden poles and bear grass.

Chapter Two

Traditional Life

The land in the Southwest provided everything the Apache needed. The desert lands provided cactus plants for food. The Apache hunted animals and gathered nuts and berries in the mountains. Some Apache planted corn and bean crops in the rich soil near rivers. The Apache moved into the low river valleys during the winter and returned to the mountains in the summer.

Shelter

Some Apache settled on the Great Plains east of the Rocky Mountains. They followed buffalo herds. Like many Plains Indians, the Eastern Apache lived in cone-shaped shelters called tepees. Buffalo were the main source of food, shelter, and clothing for these Apache.

The Western Apache lived in round huts called wickiups. The Apache made wickiup frames by pushing poles into the ground. They then bent and tied the poles together at the top. Apache women collected brush or long bear grass and tied it to the sides of the frame to build the walls. Women hung an animal skin over the door to keep out the wind and rain. The wickiups were practical for the Apache way of life. The Apache moved as often as every two weeks in their search for food. They easily could take down the wickiup and carry the poles to the next camp.

Female Roles

Women and girls spent their time gathering and preparing food. Each season provided different roots, seeds, berries, or fruits. Each spring, a group of women gathered the lettuce-sized heads of the agave plant. The women trimmed the spines from the heads, cooked them in a fire pit, rolled them into flat sheets, and dried them in the sun. The women also gathered strawberries, raspberries, and wild grapes in the summer. They found wild potatoes, wild onions, cactus fruit, acorns, sunflower seeds, and pine nuts in the fall.

Some women planted corn, beans, and pumpkins. When the Apache moved during summer, they left the young children and old tribe members to protect the crops.

The Mescalero Apache in New Mexico lived in tepees. Tepees were easy to put up and take down when the tribe was traveling.

Women taught girls to make flour from a mixture of wild grasses and crushed wild potatoes. Women made bread from this mixture and spread honey on top. Girls also learned to crush acorns into powder, mix the powder with meat and fat, and roll it into a ball. This mixture formed acorn dumplings. Men carried this food on hunting trips.

Women worked hard. They collected firewood and water from the rivers. They taught children how to find and cook food. Women made clothing for their families from deerskin.

Preparing deerskin took many days. First, a woman soaked the fresh deerskin for days to loosen the hair. She then scraped the skin to remove all the hair. Next, she made a paste of deer brains and fat and rubbed it into the skin to soften it. When the deerskin was soft and dry, the woman cut out shirts, skirts, and moccasins. She sewed them together with sinew, a fiber that connects muscle to bone.

Male Roles

Men hunted to provide meat and clothing for their families. Deer, antelope, elk, mountain sheep, and buffalo lived in Apache lands. Deer provided most of the meat the Apache needed. Deerskin was used for clothing. Men sometimes

killed mountain lions and used the skin to make bags for arrows.

Apache men carefully prepared before a hunt so the spirits would give them many animals. The hunters did not eat before a hunt. They believed the spirits would take pity on a hungry hunter and supply more deer. When the men arrived at the hunting grounds, they hunted alone or in pairs. They sometimes wore deer masks and smeared animal fat on their skin to hide themselves and their smell from the deer.

When men killed a deer, they skinned it and brought the meat, skin, head, and hooves back to camp. Apache men believed the hooves and head would bring good luck on the next hunt. Fresh meat was fried, grilled, or boiled for soup.

Bows and Arrows

Each man made his own arrows for hunting and for war. He selected branches, scraped them smooth, and left them to dry. He straightened the arrows and tied eagle feathers

or hawk feathers to one end. He hardened the other end in a fire and then sharpened it.

It took many days to make a new bow. Each man cut a branch from a mulberry, oak, or maple tree. He scraped,

Apache hunters were good trackers. They would hunt wild game by following fresh animal tracks.

dried, and bent the branch to the shape he wanted. He then finished the new bow in the hot ashes of a fire. After the bow was hard, the man marked it with designs that showed it belonged to him. For the string, the man used animal sinew.

Family Life

Most Apache lived in small family camps. Each family included parents, unmarried children, married daughters and their husbands, grandparents, and grandchildren. Each camp elected a leader who was brave, hardworking, fair, and generous. Some leaders were known for their skills in war or in hunting. No single leader ever spoke for all of the Apache. When the leaders met, all had an equal voice. The Apache were independent. They rarely met with bands far from their homelands.

When a young woman was ready to marry, her female relatives showed her possible husbands. The girl then chose a young man. He then sent the young woman's family presents such as horses, blankets, and deerskin. If her family accepted the presents, the couple was married. The Apache did not have a special ceremony for a wedding.

The young man came to live in the young woman's camp. The couple built a wickiup or tepee near her parents. The young man was expected to provide food for both his wife's

Pine Nut Muffins

The American Indians of the Southwest believed the piñon tree, a type of pine tree, was the oldest kind of tree in the world. The Apache collected nuts from the tree and ate them raw, roasted, and ground in many foods. These seeds were a good source of protein and fat. Apache women did not eat the nuts when they were pregnant. They feared their baby would grow too fat before it was born.

What You Need

1 cup (240 mL) ground pine nuts
½ cup (120 mL) whole wheat flour
2 teaspoons (10 mL) baking powder
½ teaspoon (2.5 mL) salt
½ cup (120 mL) water
3 tablespoons (45 mL) honey

Equipment

non-stick cooking spray
muffin tin
dry-ingredient measuring cups
measuring spoons
large mixing bowl
liquid-ingredient measuring cups
mixing spoons
pot holders

What You Do

1. Preheat oven to 350°F (180°C).
2. Spray muffin tin with non-stick cooking spray. Set aside.
3. Combine pine nuts, flour, baking powder, and salt in the mixing bowl.
4. Add water and honey and mix well.
5. Scoop about ⅓ cup (80 mL) of batter with measuring cup into prepared muffin tin.
6. Bake for 30 minutes.
7. Take muffins out of oven with pot holders and let cool.

Makes 6 muffins

family and his own. Most Apache believed a new husband should not talk to, or even look at, his mother-in-law.

Each family group hunted and gathered their own food. Some years, the people could not find enough to eat. They sometimes traded with the Pueblo Indians for corn. If the Apache had nothing to trade, they raided villages for the food they needed. Many nearby American Indians feared the Apache.

Growing Up Apache

After a baby was born, the mother placed it in a cradleboard. The child was strapped to the cradleboard for the first six or seven months of its life. Mothers carried babies on their backs as they worked. They decorated the top of the cradleboard with feathers, beads, and herbs. They believed this practice protected the baby from sickness.

After the age of six, the children began helping their mother. As they worked, she taught them the stories of the Apache people.

Young boys practiced their hunting skills on rabbits and squirrels. The boys practiced for their futures as hunters and warriors. When a young boy became good at shooting with bows and arrows, he asked to begin training as a warrior. By age 15, boys had learned about hunting and war. The older men then taught them how to survive alone.

Sunrise Ceremony

When a young Apache girl reaches puberty, the Apache hold a special ceremony to celebrate her new life as a woman. This ceremony lasts four days and brings many friends and relatives together. They give their blessing to the young woman and join in the feasts and dancing.

Relatives of the young woman give her many gifts. They sew a soft, deerskin blouse and dye it yellow. The blouse has fringes of leather and tin ornaments that jingle when the young woman dances. She wears moccasins that come up to her knees. A shell is placed on her forehead. She carries a yellow cane that reminds her that she will lead a long life and will need the cane when she is old.

The young woman dances. Her relatives sprinkle pollen on her head to promise a long life filled with many children. Finally, all the guests join in the dance to celebrate the entry of a new woman into the tribe.

When a boy was ready, the men took him on his first raid. He gathered wood and carried water for the men. He did the cooking. If a fight occurred, the warriors hid him. The boy watched the raid, but he never got hurt. After watching four raids, the boy was considered a man.

Apache Beliefs

For the Apache, the natural world was powerful. Each tree, animal, star, and plant had a spirit with its own power. The Apache believed certain men or women could use some of this power for themselves. Sometimes, the power came to a person by accident or through prayer. Other people learned the power from holy men or women called diyin. The diyin used their powers to cure illness or to predict success in war and raids.

Every Apache lived life according to the natural powers. Cattail pollen held a special life-giving power. The Apache used cattail pollen to bless babies. The pollen was also used to bless young women at the Sunrise Ceremony. The Apache honored the four directions of North, South, East, and West, which brought good power to the people. Some powers were bad. A bear might cause sickness, and snakes might cause skin problems. The diyin were called to help cure a person with bear or snake sickness.

Apache warriors sometimes painted spiritual figures on their clothing. This warrior's cloak is painted with the figure of an Apache "Ga'an," or spirit.

21

In the 1500s, Spanish explorer Francisco Vasquez de Coronado traveled as far north as Kansas in his search for gold.

Chapter Three

Spanish and Americans Bring Change

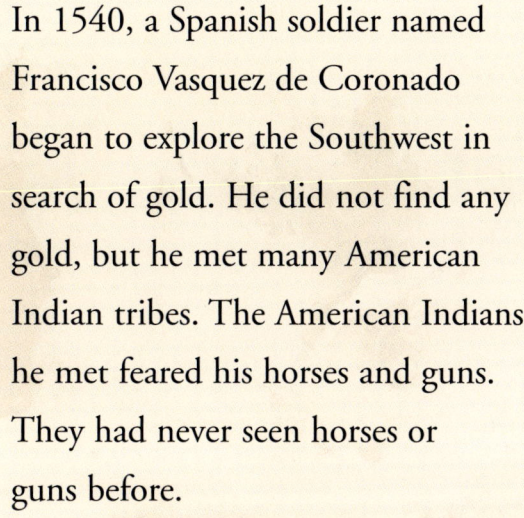

In 1540, a Spanish soldier named Francisco Vasquez de Coronado began to explore the Southwest in search of gold. He did not find any gold, but he met many American Indian tribes. The American Indians he met feared his horses and guns. They had never seen horses or guns before.

Apache Raids

The Apache lived in the mountains and were curious about Spanish settlers moving into their lands. They learned that the Spanish horses and cattle were good to eat.

The Apache were good raiders. Small family groups planned raids to steal Spanish animals for food. The raiders stole horses or cattle and escaped back to their camp before the Spanish noticed the animals were gone.

Spanish settlers became angry about the raids. Some tried to teach the Apache to settle into villages. In the 1600s, Spanish leaders realized the Apache would never settle into villages. The Spanish captured the Apache and sent them to Mexico to work without pay in mines and factories. Whenever an Apache was captured, other tribe members took Spanish settlers and their children as captives. They adopted the Spanish children and raised them as their own.

Although the Apache still liked horses for food, they saw how horses could be used for moving their camps. Around 1630, some Pueblo Indians joined the Apache and taught the Apache how to ride horses. The Apache were able to move quickly and began using the horses during raids.

From 1600 until the mid-1800s, the Apache continued to raid towns. The raiders were fearless. They were willing to die in battle rather than be captured.

Mexico

In 1821, Mexico declared itself independent from Spain. For the next 27 years, Mexico governed what is now the state of New Mexico. The Mexicans were afraid of the Apache and believed the Apache should be killed. Mexico passed a law to pay money to anyone who killed an Apache.

Apache warriors made many raids on Spanish settlements. They, like Geronimo pictured here, often took horses and cattle during the raids.

In 1846, the United States went to war with Mexico over land. In 1848, the United States and Mexico signed the Treaty of Guadalupe Hidalgo. The treaty ended the Mexican War (1846–1848). Under this agreement, Mexico sold Texas, California, Nevada, Utah, and parts of Arizona, New Mexico, Colorado, and Wyoming to the United States for $15 million.

The Apache were friendly to the United States at first. They were happy the Americans had fought against the Mexicans. The Apache still raided places in Mexico for cattle and horses. The U.S. government promised to stop these raids in the Treaty of Guadalupe Hidalgo. The U.S. government made plans to move the Apache onto reservations to stop the raids.

More settlers came to New Mexico and Arizona in the mid-1800s. In 1848, settlers discovered gold in California. The road from the eastern United States to California passed through Apache lands. The California gold rush brought many settlers through New Mexico. The Apache saw their homelands become smaller as settlers claimed Apache lands. The Apache ran out of food. They finally agreed to go to reservations because the U.S. government promised them food.

Cochise

In the 1860s, Cochise was a popular leader of some Apache in southern Arizona. In 1861, some Apache who were not with

Cochise attacked a settler in Arizona. They took his cattle and captured his young son. The settler accused Cochise of taking his son.

U.S. soldiers told Cochise to bring the boy back. Cochise claimed he did not know about the raid or the boy.

Cochise led many attacks against the U.S. Army between 1863 and 1872.

The soldiers planned to arrest Cochise and his men anyway. Cochise escaped, but the soldiers arrested six of his men.

Cochise wanted his men back. He captured settlers and offered to trade them for his men. The soldiers wanted to trade their Apache prisoners for the boy and the settlers. Cochise did not understand why the soldiers did not believe him when he said he did not have the boy. He killed his prisoners, and the soldiers killed their prisoners. The peace between the United States and the Apache was over.

Relocation

From 1848 to 1886, the U.S. government made arrangements to move the Apache to reservations. These reservations were not on Apache homelands. The reservations did not allow the Apache to lead their nomadic lifestyle. Some Apache did not like the reservation land and left for their old homelands. They continued to raid towns in Mexico and the United States.

In September 1886, U.S. soldiers gave Apache leader Geronimo a choice. If he surrendered, the U.S. government would send the Apache to a prison in Florida for two years. If he did not, the soldiers would fight his people until all were dead. Geronimo wanted his people to survive, even if they had to move to Florida. Geronimo and 37 warriors surrendered. His band and other Apache prisoners boarded trains for Florida.

Geronimo

In 1829, Geronimo was born in what is now southeastern Arizona. He was a member of the Chiricahua band of Apache. He came from a family of eight. At age 17, Geronimo began to go on raids. He became a fearless warrior.

In 1881, U.S. soldiers arrested Geronimo and sent him to the San Carlos Reservation in Arizona. He escaped to Mexico with some followers. For five years, Geronimo and his men raided Mexican and U.S. towns along the U.S.-Mexican border.

In 1886, U.S. Army General Nelson Miles and 5,000 soldiers began to look for Geronimo. It took months for Miles, Apache scouts, and U.S. soldiers to find and capture Geronimo and his band.

After Geronimo's surrender, nearly 400 Chiricahua Apache, including Geronimo, were sent to a prison in St. Augustine, Florida. Later, the prisoners were moved to Alabama and finally to Fort Sill in Oklahoma. In 1909, Geronimo died at Fort Sill without ever seeing Arizona again.

In the late 1800s, some Apache children were sent to boarding schools. They were forced to cut their hair and dress in American-style clothing.

Chapter Four

The Apache Today

The Apache survived years of war and a forced move to reservation lands. The reservation lands were not good for farming. The Apache often did not have enough food and clothing. Some Apache children were sent by the U.S. government to boarding schools in the eastern United States. The schools forced the children to speak English and dress in American-style clothing. They also had to cut their hair in styles popular with white people of that time.

In spite of these troubles, the Apache have a strong identity today. All Apache reservations have tribal councils that control how the land is used and where the money is spent. The Apache people have survived with a sense of what it means to be Apache.

Apache Reservations

The three Apache reservations in Arizona are developing their natural resources to provide income for band members. The Fort Apache Reservation has good grasslands for ranching. The mountains provide wood for the reservation's lumber mill. Tourists can ski, hunt, and fish in the mountains.

Many of the Fort Apache men and women are fire fighters. They work for the U.S. Forest Service during the summer forest fire season.

The San Carlos and Tonto Reservations are smaller than the Fort Apache Reservation. The San Carlos Reservation has an Apache Cultural Center. Visitors to the center can

learn more about the history of the Apache and the reservation. The San Carlos Reservation also holds a rodeo and fair each November. Both the San Carlos and Tonto Reservations run casinos.

The Fort Apache Timber Company harvests trees from more than 800,000 acres (324,000 hectares) of tribal forest land. The forest land is on the Fort Apache Reservation.

One of New Mexico's best golf courses is at Ruidoso's Inn of the Mountain Gods on the Mescalero Apache Reservation.

Mildred Cleghorn

In 1910, Mildred Cleghorn was born at Fort Sill, Oklahoma. For the first three years of her life, the U.S. government held her family prisoner. When her family was released in 1913, they settled on a farm near Apache, Oklahoma.

As a girl in Oklahoma, Cleghorn went to public schools, but no other American Indian children attended with her. She begged her parents to allow her to go to an American Indian school in Lawrence, Kansas. She wanted to meet other American Indians her own age.

In 1941, she graduated from college with a degree in home economics. She wanted to work with American Indian families on the reservations to improve their lives.

From 1977 until 1995, Cleghorn served as the chairwoman of the Fort Sill Apache Indian Tribal Council. In 1989, the leaders of the American Indian Exposition in Oklahoma chose Cleghorn as Indian of the Year. This honor is given to an American Indian who works to help other American Indians. Cleghorn was 86 years old when she died in a car accident in 1997.

The two reservations in New Mexico are located on mountain lands rich with natural resources. Both the Jicarilla and the Mescalero Reservations offer tourists skiing, hunting, and fishing. The Jicarilla Apache raise cattle. The Jicarilla Reservation is well known for its mule deer and elk hunting. The Mescalero Reservation has a well-known golf course and a casino.

In 1886, the U.S. government sent the Chiricahua Apache to a prison in Florida.

The two Apache bands in Oklahoma are the smallest of the Apache communities. The Chiricahua Apache were sent to Oklahoma after eight years of prison in Florida. In 1913, the U.S. government offered the Chiricahua a choice. They could stay in Oklahoma or move to the Mescalero Reservation. Most of the Apache chose to go to the Mescalero Reservation on their New Mexico homelands, but 87 stayed in Oklahoma. This small group formed the Fort Sill Apache band. They do not live on a reservation but instead have farms near Apache, Oklahoma.

The group once known as the Kiowa-Apache formed a separate band known as the Apache Tribe of Oklahoma. They share their reservation with the Kiowa and the Comanche Nations. Though the Oklahoma Apache live far from the other Apache communities, some visit New Mexico and Arizona for tribal ceremonies.

Apache dancers take part in the War Dance during the Apache Mescal Roast in New Mexico.

Chapter Five

Sharing the Traditions

The Apache have adapted to the U.S. way of life, but they also work to preserve their traditional ways. About 75 percent of the people on the Arizona and Mescalero reservations speak the Apache language. Elementary school students use Mescalero and Western Apache dictionaries to learn to read and write Apache. The Jicarilla are also working on a dictionary, and more than 50 percent of the band speaks Apache. The Oklahoma bands no longer speak Apache, though some still understand it.

Culture and Heritage

Many Apache continue to practice their traditional ceremonies and beliefs. Most Apache in Arizona and New Mexico still celebrate the Sunrise Ceremony. They often combine this ceremony with an annual tribal celebration that brings families together for dancing, races, feasts, and a rodeo.

In 1993, the Fort Apache band in Arizona was the first American Indian group to create a tourist park that presents history from the American Indian point of view. The Fort

The Fort Apache Cultural Center shows visitors the artwork and crafts of the White Mountain Apache.

Apache Ga'an

In Apache traditional stories, the Creator sent the mountain spirits, called Ga'an, to teach the people how to live a holy life. The Ga'an taught them to respect the animals they hunted, to be kind to each other and the poor, and to take care of the land. They also brought ceremonies to heal the sick and to pray to the Creator.

During the Sunrise Ceremony for young girls, dancers dress up as the Ga'an to bring good health and a long life to the girl. Four dancers represent the four compass directions. They wear buckskin skirts and large headdresses made of painted wood. Their bodies are painted by a medicine man with designs that represent lightning, mountains, and animals.

Today, the Ga'an sometimes dance for tourists. They are called Crown Dancers because of their large headdresses. The dance is also called the Dance of the Mountain Spirits. But their most important duty is to help bring young Apache girls into adulthood. The Ga'an dancers help the Apache celebrate their traditions and remember their old ways.

Apache Historic Park offers tours of historic buildings. Nearby, the Apache Cultural Center and Museum preserves recorded songs and stories, photographs, crafts, and artwork of the White Mountain Apache. At the Mescalero Cultural Center in New Mexico, visitors can see historic photographs, traditional clothing, and videos of the Apache story.

After the U.S. government sent them to reservations, the Apache began selling their baskets and deerskin moccasins to tourists. Selling crafts helped the Apache earn money. The Apache were known for the baskets they wove from willow, yucca, cottonwood, or sumac plants.

At the San Carlos Apache Cultural Center in Arizona, the band has combined historic exhibits and an artists' center. Visitors can learn about basketmaking, beadwork, leatherwork, and other traditional crafts. They also can see work by modern Apache artists.

The cultural centers and celebrations attract both young and old Apache. The children learn to dance from their parents. They learn to speak Apache in school and from their families. Parents today tell the same stories as their Apache ancestors. The Apache believe their children need to be part of the American way of life. The Apache also want their children to remember the history and culture of the Apache.

Baskets

Apache women are known for their skill at making baskets. Traditional Apache women made three kinds of baskets from the stems and branches of yucca, sumac, cottonwood or willow trees. They made small, flat trays used for separating grains and seeds. A tall basket with a flat bottom was called a burden basket. Women used these baskets to carry heavy loads of firewood and agave.

In the dry lands of the Southwest, women also made baskets to carry water. To make them, they wove strips of sumac tightly until they had a tall basket. Next, they used a stick to smear the heated sappy pitch of a pine tree on the outside and inside of the basket. When this sticky pitch cooled, the basket would hold water. The pitch cooled quickly and the baskets could be used the same day. If a basket began to leak, the women reheated the pitch and smeared it again to cover the hole.

Apache Timeline

| 1000–1500 | 1540 | 1590s | 1821 |

- **1540**: Coronado explores the land of the Apache.
- **1821**: Mexico declares independence from Spain.
- **1000–1500**: Apache move from Canada to the Great Plains and the Southwest.
- **1590s**: The Spanish settle in the Southwest.

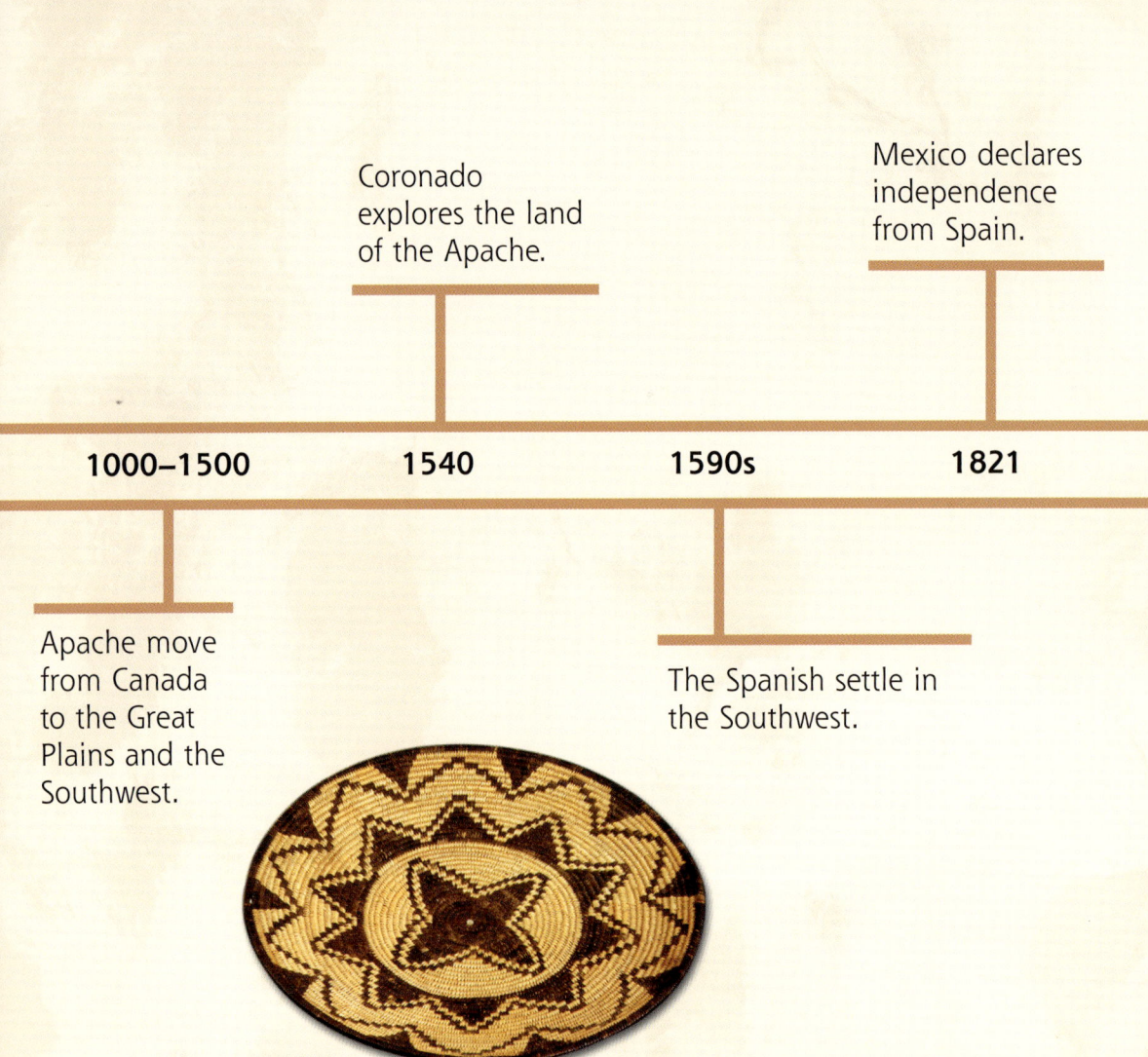

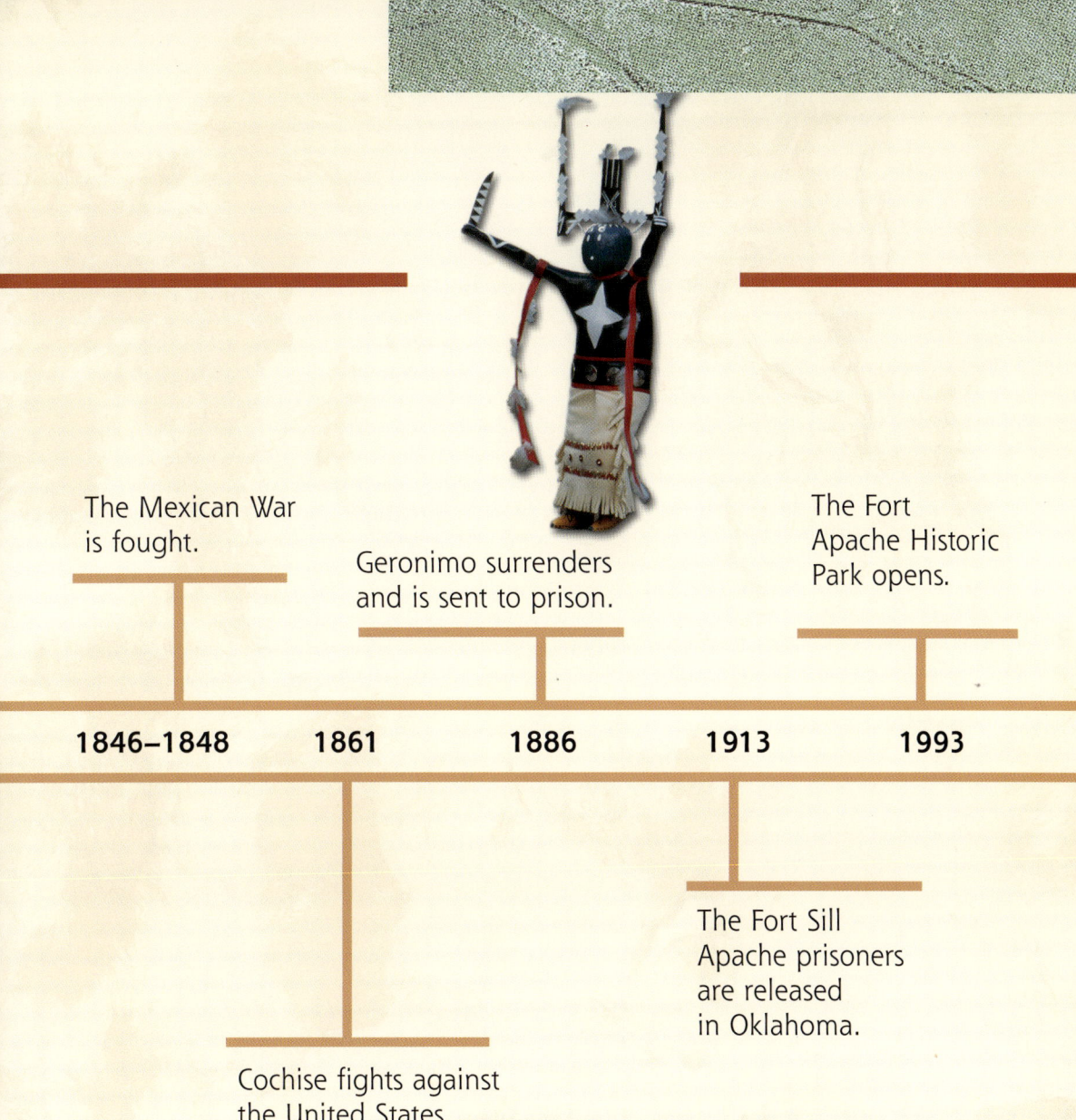

The Mexican War is fought.

Geronimo surrenders and is sent to prison.

The Fort Apache Historic Park opens.

1846–1848 **1861** **1886** **1913** **1993**

Cochise fights against the United States.

The Fort Sill Apache prisoners are released in Oklahoma.

45

Glossary

agave (uh-GAH-vay)—a plant with long pointed leaves found in the deserts of the Southwest; the Apache used the agave plant for food.

diyin (DEE-in)—a religious leader of the Apache

nomad (NOH-mad)—a person who travels from place to place to find food and water

pollen (POL-uhn)—tiny grains that flowers produce

puberty (PYOO-bur-tee)—the time when a child's body becomes more like an adult's body

wickiup (WIK-ee-uhp)—a rounded Apache home made with pole frames and covered with grass

For Further Reading

Bial, Raymond. *The Apache.* Lifeways. New York: Benchmark Books, 2001.

Gaines, Richard. *The Apache.* Native Americans. Edina, Minn.: Abdo, 2000.

Lund, Bill. *The Apache Indians.* Native Peoples. Mankato, Minn.: Bridgestone Books, 1998.

Press, Petra. *The Apache.* First Reports. Minneapolis: Compass Point Books, 2002.

Places to Write & Visit

Fort Apache Historic Park
P.O. Box 628
Fort Apache, AZ 85926

Jicarilla Apache Tribe
P.O. Box 507
Dulce, NM 87528

Mescalero Apache Tribe
P.O. Box 227
Mescalero, NM 88340

San Carlos Apache Cultural Center
P.O. Box 760
Peridot, AZ 85542

Internet Sites

Track down many sites about the Apache.
Visit the FACT HOUND at http://www.facthound.com

IT IS EASY! IT IS FUN!

1) Go to *http://www.facthound.com*
2) Type in: 0736815635
3) Click on "FETCH IT" and FACT HOUND will find several links hand-picked by our editors.

Relax and let our pal FACT HOUND do the research for you!

Index

baskets, 42, 43
beliefs, 20, 40, 41
boarding schools, 30, 31
bows and arrows, 14–16, 18

casinos, 7, 33, 35
children, 7, 11, 12, 16, 18, 19, 20, 24, 30, 31, 35, 42
Cleghorn, Mildred, 35
clothing, 4, 10, 12, 21, 30, 31, 41, 42
Cochise, 26–28
Coronado, Francisco Vasquez de, 22, 23
cradleboard, 18

diyin, 20

Eastern Apache, 6–7, 10
    Chiricahua Apache, 7, 29, 36, 37
    Jicarilla Apache, 7, 35, 39
    Kiowa-Apache, 7, 37
    Lipan Apache, 7
    Mescalero Apache, 4, 7, 11, 34, 35, 39, 42

family, 16, 18, 19, 24, 42
farming, 7, 9, 11, 31
food, 9, 10–12, 14, 16, 17, 18, 24, 26, 31
Fort Sill, 29, 35, 37

Ga'an, 21, 41
Geronimo, 25, 28, 29
golf course, 34, 35

horses, 6, 16, 23, 24, 25, 26
hunting, 6, 7, 9, 12, 14, 15, 16, 18, 35

language, 6, 7, 39
lumber, 32, 33

men's traditional roles, 12, 14–16, 18
Mexicans, 6, 7, 25–26
Mexican War, 26

nomads, 6, 28

pollen, 19, 20

raid, 6, 18, 20, 24, 25, 26, 28, 29
reservations, 7, 26, 28, 29, 31, 32–33, 34, 35, 37, 39, 42

Spanish, 5, 6, 7, 22, 23, 24, 25
Sunrise Ceremony, 19, 20, 40, 41

tepees, 10, 11
tourism, 7, 32, 35, 40, 41, 42
Treaty of Guadalupe Hidalgo, 26

U.S. Army, 27–28, 29
U.S. government, 6, 7, 26, 28, 31, 35, 36, 37, 42

warrior, 18, 20, 21, 25, 28, 29
Western Apache, 6–7, 8, 10, 39
    San Carlos Apache, 7, 42
    Tonto Apache, 7
    White Mountain Apache, 7, 40, 42
wickiup, 8, 10, 16
women's traditional roles, 10–12, 16